Pebble® Plus

Plant Life Cycles

The Life Cycle of a Sunflower

by Linda Tagliaferro

Consulting Editor: Gail Saunders-Smith, PhD

Consultant: Judson R. Scott, Current President
American Society of Consulting Arborists

Capstone
press®
Mankato, Minnesota

Pebble Plus is published by Capstone Press,
151 Good Counsel Drive, P.O. Box 669, Mankato, Minnesota 56002.
www.capstonepress.com

1 2 3 4 5 6 12 11 10 09 08 07

Library of Congress Cataloging-in-Publication Data
Tagliaferro, Linda.
    The life cycle of a sunflower / by Linda Tagliaferro.
    p. cm.—(Pebble Plus. Plant life cycles)
    Summary: "Simple text and photographs present the life cycle of a sunflower plant from seed
to adult"—Provided by publisher.
    Includes bibliographical references and index.
    ISBN-13: 978-0-7368-6714-6 (hardcover)
    ISBN-10: 0-7368-6714-7 (hardcover)
    1. Sunflowers—Juvenile literature. 2. Sunflowers—Life cycles—Juvenile literature. I. Title. II. Series.
QK495.C74T34 2007
583'.99—dc22   2006020944

Editorial Credits
Sarah L. Schuette, editor; Bobbi J. Wyss, set designer; Jo Miller, photo researcher/photo editor

Photo Credits
Dwight R. Kuhn, cover (seeds, seedling), 5, 7, 9, 11, 13, 15 (inset), 20 (seeds)
Grant Heilman Photography/Tom Hovland, 15
Shutterstock/Alexander Romanovich, 21 (sunflowers); ARTEKI, cover (sunflower); Evon Lim Seo Ling, 20
    (sprouting seed); GemPhoto, 19; Graca Victoria, cover (soil); Nancy Tunison, 21 (flower bud)
Unicorn Stock Photos/Eric R. Berndt, 17

Note to Parents and Teachers

The Plant Life Cycles set supports national science standards related to plant and animal
life cycles. This book describes and illustrates the life cycle of a sunflower. The images
support early readers in understanding the text. The repetition of words and phrases
helps early readers learn new words. This book also introduces early readers to subject-
specific vocabulary words, which are defined in the Glossary section. Early readers may
need assistance to read some words and to use the Table of Contents, Glossary, Read
More, Internet Sites, and Index sections of the book.

Table of Contents

Sunflower Seeds

How do sunflowers grow?
Sunflowers grow from the
seeds of the sunflower plant.

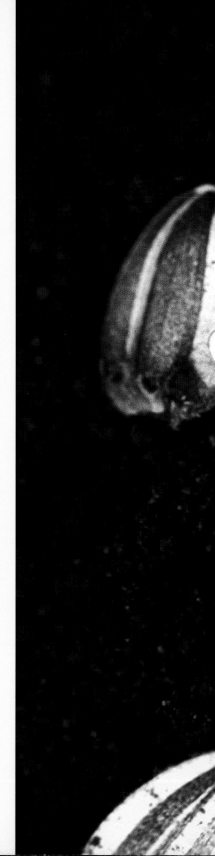

5

Sunflower seeds need sunlight,
soil, water, and warmth.
Then they sprout.

Growing

Stems peek out
on top of the soil.
Small leaves grow
on the stems.

Stems fill with more leaves
and branches.

Leaves make food for plants.

Flower buds form
on the branches.
Then the buds open.

Sunflowers!

Sunflowers bloom.

They move to face the sun.

Seeds form inside the flowers.

In fall, sunflowers bend
and their seeds scatter.

Starting Over

Next year,

new sunflowers grow.

The life cycle continues.

How Sunflowers Grow

seeds

sprouting seed

flower bud

sunflower

Glossary

branch—the part of a plant or tree that grows out of the main stem like an arm

life cycle—the stages in the life of a plant that include sprouting, reproducing, and dying

scatter—to be thrown or to fall over a wide area

seed—the part of a flowering plant that can grow into a new plant

soil—the dirt where plants grow; most plants get their food and water from the soil.

sprout—to grow, appear, or develop quickly

stem—the long main part of a plant that makes leaves

Read More

Cooper, Jason. *Sunflower.* Life Cycles. Vero Beach, Fla.: Rourke, 2004.

Ganeri, Anita. *From Seed to Sunflower.* How Living Things Grow. Chicago: Heinemann, 2006.

Godwin, Sam. *A Seed in Need: A First Look at the Plant Cycle.* First Look: Science. Minneapolis: Picture Window Books, 2005.

Parker, Victoria. *Life as a Sunflower.* Life as. Chicago: Raintree, 2004.

Internet Sites

FactHound offers a safe, fun way to find Internet sites related to this book. All of the sites on FactHound have been researched by our staff.

Here's how:

1. Visit *www.facthound.com*

2. Choose your grade level.

3. Type in this book ID **0736867147** for age-appropriate sites. You may also browse subjects by clicking on letters, or by clicking on pictures and words.

4. Click on the **Fetch It** button.

FactHound will fetch the best sites for you!

Index

Word Count: 90
Grade: 1
Early-Intervention Level: 13